WRITTEN BY
VICKI TASHMAN

ILLUSTRATED BY
WENDY ALL

This Book Belongs To:

Published by Historical Tails www.HistoricalTails.com

This is a work of historical fiction. That means all the names, places, and time period are real but the story, conversations and thoughts are fiction.

Cover and book illustrations by Wendy All copyright ©2019. All rights reserved.
www.WendyAll.com
Cover and book design by Nate Myers.

Ebook ISBN: 978-0-9972094-4-0
Paperback ISBN: 978-0-9972094-3-3

Library of Congress Control Number: 2019900219

CHAPTER 1

"I want to chase you again, Lory!" Dash shouted.
"All right," said Lory. "One more time."

So once again the dog chased the parrot around the elegant room and right onto the lap of Queen Victoria.

"You are both so sweet!" Victoria said, laughing.

When Victoria was 13 years old, Dash arrived as a young dog. He was intended as a present for Victoria's mother, the Duchess of Kent. But with one look at his big brown eyes and floppy ears Victoria fell in love with him. Dash slept in her room every night and was with her always.

In 1837, Victoria was eighteen years old when her uncle, King William IV*, died. Victoria was now the Queen of the United Kingdom of Great Britain and Ireland. She was too young to be Queen but she was ready.

*Victoria's Uncle was King William the Fourth. They use Roman numerals.

The young queen's palace was a playful place. Victoria loved animals and she had many of them.

There was Lory the colorful parrot*,

Islay*, a grumpy gray* terrier

and Dash the Spaniel.

*The British spell "colorful" like "colourful," pronounce "Islay" like "eye-la" and they spell "gray" like "grey."

Many other people lived in the palace but Victoria was the only one Dash wanted to be with. He barked when anyone came near her.

He even barked at Victoria's nanny*, the Baroness Lehzen, and her mother, the Duchess of Kent.

*The Baroness was young Victoria's nanny and continued to live in the palace, taking care of Victoria's children.

Though Dash thought Lory was lots of fun, he did not like Islay. Islay always tried to sit on Victoria's lap and that was Dash's special place. Dash growled at him whenever he came near Victoria.

"You don't need to sit on her lap," Dash said to him. "I'm her favorite*, not you!"

"She loves me too," Islay said sadly.

* The British spell the word "favorite" like "favourite."

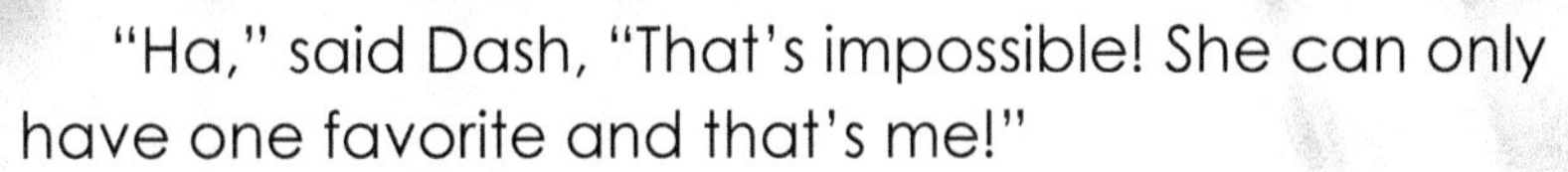

“Ha,” said Dash, “That’s impossible! She can only have one favorite and that’s me!”

All Victoria could hear was barking and growling. “Oh, Dashy,” she told him, stroking his ears. “It’s all right.”

But Lory understood what they were fighting about. She cocked her head to the side and squawked, “Dash, you have no reason to be jealous.”

CHAPTER 2

Dash was happy lying on Victoria's bed. When Victoria cuddled him, scratched his neck and twirled his ear, he rolled onto his back for a belly rub.

"Stay still, Dashy," she said. "I'm drawing your cute little nose."

Dash stayed still until she finished drawing.

"Prince Albert is coming from Coburg*, Dash," she said. "Please don't bark at him. He's very nice."

Dash wasn't sure who Prince Albert from Coburg was, but he didn't like the idea of anyone coming near Victoria so he barked.

Victoria smiled and touched the tip of his nose with her pencil. "I'm twenty now and my government wishes** me to marry. He may be the one," Victoria said.

Dash kissed her cheek with a big sloppy lick.

*Coburg is a town in what is today's Germany.

** "wishes" means "wants."

CHAPTER 3

A couple of days later there was a knock on the door and in came Victoria's butler.

"Your Majesty has a visitor," he announced. "Prince Albert from Coburg is here."

"Oh, thank you! Show him to the Great Room. I'll be there shortly," Victoria replied.

She looked at herself in the mirror, gathered up her skirts and ran out the door.

Dash ran after her, barking. He thought it was time for their walk in the garden. But instead of going outside, he stopped. A man was walking up the stairs.

"Who is this person?" thought Dash. "And what about our walk?"

Prince Albert kneeled in front of Victoria and gave her hand a kiss. Dash ran to her side.

"Arf, arf, arf!"

"Let's go into the Great Room," Victoria said.

Dash continued to bark. Lory was perched in his cage and he started squawking. Islay was lying by the fireplace and he started barking too.

"Squawk, squawk, squawk!"

"Woof, woof, woof!"

"Arf, arf, arf!"

"It sounds like a zoo in here!" the prince laughed. He looked down at Dash, who was growling.

"Who do we have here?" asked Albert

"This is my dog Dash," said Victoria and she scooped him into her arms.

Albert held out a hand for Dash to sniff. "It's all right, Dash," said Albert. "I'm a friend of the Queen."

Albert looked into Victoria's eyes and they both blushed.

Dash growled again.

"Dash, my sweet, shhhh," she whispered, and she gave Dash a hug.

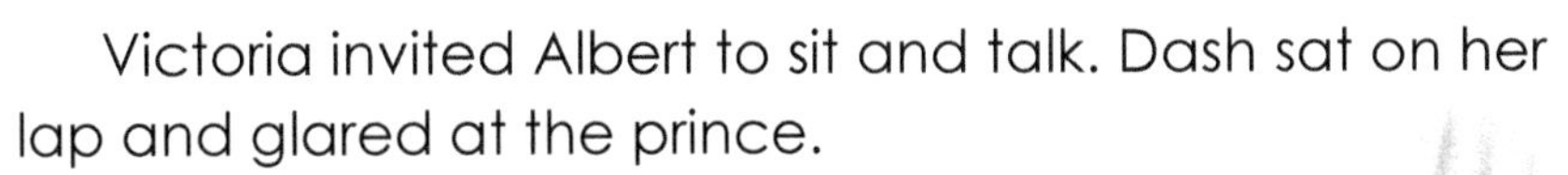

Victoria invited Albert to sit and talk. Dash sat on her lap and glared at the prince.

"How long will you be visiting?" Victoria asked.

"Just a fortnight*," he replied. "I'd like to see the countryside."

*"Fortnight" means two weeks.

"We can go for a ride," Victoria said.

"Why is she inviting Albert to ride with us?" Dash wondered. "We always ride alone."

"Arf, arf, arf!"

"Don't worry, Dashy," Victoria said. "You can come with us."

Victoria's soothing caress made Dash relax and soon he felt sleepy.

"Would you take me on a tour of the Houses of Parliament, Your Majesty?" Albert asked. "I'd love to see the buildings."

Dash's eyelids grew heavier.

"Of course, Albert," Victoria replied. "We can go next week when the government is in session."

Dash closed his eyes. Soon he was asleep, very comfortable on Victoria's lap. Quietly Albert kneeled in front of Victoria and kissed her hand again.

"Let's not wake Dash," he said with a smile.

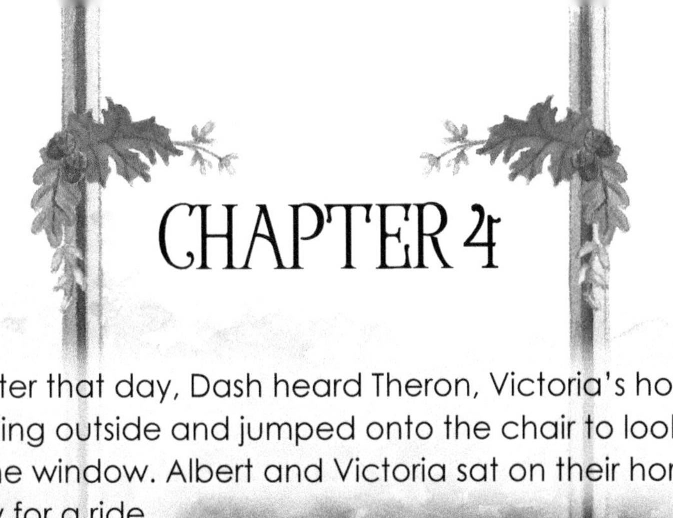

CHAPTER 4

Later that day, Dash heard Theron, Victoria's horse, neighing outside and jumped onto the chair to look out the window. Albert and Victoria sat on their horses ready for a ride.

Dash started to whine. Did Victoria love him? It seemed like she loved Albert now. How could she love him AND Albert at the same time?

"I usually go riding with Victoria!" he said to Lory. "I thought I was her favorite."

"Victoria loves many animals and people, Dash," Lory replied.

"But how can that be? She loves me with all her heart. She's told me so!"

Dash ran out of the room, down the stairs and out the door of the palace.

"Poor Dash," thought Lory. "He needs to learn a lesson in love."

Dash ran as fast as he could behind the horses. "Arf, arf, arf! I have to scare away the foxes. Theron doesn't like them. I have to protect Victoria."

Victoria heard him barking. "That's Dash!" She turned around and saw him on the pathway far behind them.

"Let's slow down a bit so he can catch up," said Albert.

Dash knew he could take a shortcut to the riding path by jumping across a small stream. But, when he landed, he felt something snap on his leg.

CHAPTER 5

Dash was caught in a trap. No matter how he tried to wriggle out of it, he couldn't. "Arf, arf, arf!" He barked until he was too tired to bark anymore.

Victoria heard him. "Albert, something has happened to Dash. Where is he?" "Dashy! Dashy!" she called frantically.

Albert jumped off his horse and ran into the wooded area near the stream. He found Dash lying in a heap.

"Here he is, Victoria!" he yelled. "We must get him back to the palace and send for a veterinarian!"

Albert freed Dash's leg from the trap, picked him up and jumped onto his horse. Dash didn't growl. He felt safe in Albert's arms. They galloped back to the palace.

CHAPTER 6

Dash was so tired he didn't mind when the veterinarian wrapped his leg with a bandage. Victoria and Albert watched fearfully.

"Is he going to be all right?" said Victoria.

"Yes, he will," said the vet. "But he needs some rest. No more running in the woods for a while."

Victoria's lip began to tremble. "I can't live without him, Albert," she said. She leaned down to kiss Dash's nose and cried.

Albert gave her arm a squeeze. "If you can't live without him, then I can't either." Victoria looked up at him and smiled.

From her perch, Lory watched them and thought, "If only Dash could see how much Victoria loves him, he wouldn't be troubled."

CHAPTER 7

Albert sat next to Dash's pillow stroking the dog's head. Dash opened his eyes a little bit. "Shhh," said Albert. "Everything is fine."

Dash closed his eyes and went back to sleep.

Albert took out his pen and paper and drew Dash sleeping. He drew Dash's little nose and fluffy tail. "It's all right Dashy," he said. "You'll be right as rain."*

*"You'll be right as rain" means "You'll be better soon."

CHAPTER 8

The next day Dash opened his eyes and saw the bandage on his leg. "What is this?" He started to lick it.

"Stop, Dash!" Victoria yelled. "Don't lick your bandage." And she patted his head. "You gave me a big fright*," she said, nuzzling his fur. "I thought you would die." Then she began to cry.

Dash stopped licking his bandage and licked her face instead.

* A "fright" is the same as a scare.

"Yes, Dash, a terrible fright," said a deep voice.

Dash saw Albert sitting next to the bed. He started to growl. Then he remembered that Albert had freed him from the trap, carried him back to the house and soothed him.

Suddenly Dash smelled something delicious.

"Here, boy," Albert said. "Try a bit of this. I think you'll like it." He held out his hand and Dash sniffed the pieces of meat he was holding out to him. He slowly took one from Albert's hand.

"Hmmm," Dash thought, "this is good!" Islay watched with concern.

"Islay, why don't you take one too," Dash said. "I think you'll like it."

"Dash, look at what Albert drew," said Victoria. She held up the sketch Albert had been working on. "It's you!" said Victoria. "It's very clever*." Victoria looked at Albert with a big smile.

* "Clever" means "good."

Dash looked up at Victoria and Albert. "She really fancies* him," Dash thought.

"Well at least he's eating," said Victoria happily.

"Why don't we take him for a ride tomorrow and I will hold him," Albert said.

"That sounds splendid," Dash thought to himself.

*"Fancies" means to like someone.

CHAPTER 9

Dash loved the feeling of wet mud on his paws when he followed Victoria's horse. But today he wasn't running in the mud. He sat in the saddle with Albert, flying along with the wind in his face.

He looked up at Albert and nuzzled into his arms. Next to them, Victoria was riding on Theron. Dash felt safe and loved. He knew he was Victoria AND Albert's special favorite.

And they were both his special favorites, too.

VARIOUS FACTS

Queen Victoria was born on May 24, 1819. Her father was Prince Edward, Duke of Kent and Strathearn. Her mother was Princess Victoria of Saxe-Coburg-Saalfeld. Dash was born in 1830 and was given to Victoria in 1833, Victoria was 14. She had a very lonely childhood, was kept in the Palace with no friends, so Dash became her best friend.

When Victoria was 13 years old, she was given a diary. She wrote in her diary every day until just before she passed away. She called them her "journals" and there are 121 of them. Some of the information presented in this book was found in her diary. You can see pictures of some of the pages of her diary on the Historical Tails website.

Victoria was known for her sketches and artistic talent. She sketched Dash many times. You can see a picture of one of her sketches in the back of this book.

Victoria became Queen when her Uncle, King William IV died. She was only 18 years old. Her birth name was Alexandrina Victoria but wanted to be known as Queen Victoria. She was Queen for 63 years! That was the longest ever for a British Monarch. She was known for the time period that was named after her, the Victorian era.

Victoria first met her cousin Prince Albert when she was 17 years old. She liked him but wasn't ready to marry. He lived in Germany and they wrote letters to each other for three years. Finally, in 1839, she asked him to visit her in England. They fell in love and the Queen asked him to marry her (Albert couldn't propose to Victoria because she was Queen, so she asked him). They were married 4 months later, in February 1840. She was the first bride to wear white.

Victoria had many pets in her lifetime. She loved her dogs, horses and birds but Dash was her favorite. In 1839, she had Dash (a King Charles Spaniel), Islay (some sources say a Skye Terrier and some sources say a Cairn Terrier) and Lory. Lory was (by the illustrator's research) confirmed to be an Eclectus Parrot. They are affectionate, friendly and smart, and can live up to forty years. Female Eclectus Parrots are red, whereas the males are green. No other species of parrot has this unusual quality. Victoria also had 2 other dogs not portrayed in this book, Hector (a mastiff) and Nero (a Greyhound).

For more information about Dash and Victoria, please visit the Historical Tails website at http://www.historicaltails.com

Queen Victoria was known for her drawing and painting talents. She took art lessons as a young girl and practiced her talents her entire life. This drawing of Dash was done in 1833 when Victoria was 14 years old.

This painting of Princess Victoria was done in 1833 when she was 13 years old. The artist was Sir George Hayter. Victoria is holding a rose and standing next to a table with books and a globe. At her feet is Dash holding one of her gloves.

ABOUT THE AUTHOR AND ILLUSTRATOR

Vicki Tashman has always loved historical fiction. Her first children's book is about Thomas Jefferson and his dog, Buzzy. Her second book is about Queen Victoria and her dog, Dash. Vicki is a member of the Society of Children's Book Writers and Illustrators (SCBWI), Independent Writers of Southern Calif (IWOSC) and The Independent Book Publishers Association (IBPA). She lives in Los Angeles with her husband and golden retriever, Georgia.

Wendy All is a toy designer and illustrator. Her career includes Mattel, (Girl's Toys and Barbie) Hasbro, (My Little Pony, *Star Wars, Jurassic Park*) and Disney Consumer Products (Disney Princesses, Winnie-the-Pooh, and others) plus numerous children's books with licensed product tie-ins. She dabbles in costume design. She and her husband, Jay, live with two big dogs, Ravel and Maya. Her favorite things to draw are animals and costumes.

To download your free coloring pages and to subscribe to our email list, please visit:
https://www.historicaltails.com/free-coloring-download-page/

CPSIA information can be obtained
at www.ICGtesting.com
Printed in the USA
BVHW090007230519
549085BV00005B/35/P